MW01078173

The MILKMAN

CAROL FOSKETT CORDSEN

illustrated by DOUGLAS B. JONES

Dutton Children's Books

NEW YORK

To my parents, my husband, and my children.
I love you all.

C.F.C.

For my mother and father

D.B.J.

DUTTON CHILDREN'S BOOKS
A division of Penguin Young Readers Group

Published by the Penguin Group
Penguin Group (USA) Inc., 375 Hudson Street, New York, New York 10014, U.S.A.
Penguin Group (Canada), 10 Alcorn Avenue, Toronto, Ontario, Canada M4V 3B2
(a division of Pearson Penguin Canada Inc.)
Penguin Books Ltd, 80 Strand, London WC2R 0RL, England
Penguin Ireland, 25 St Stephen's Green, Dublin 2, Ireland
(a division of Penguin Books Ltd)
Penguin Group (Australia), 250 Camberwell Road, Camberwell, Victoria 3124, Australia
(a division of Pearson Australia Group Pty Ltd)
Penguin Books India Pvt Ltd, 11 Community Centre, Panchsheel Park, New Delhi—110 017, India
Penguin Group (NZ), Cnr Airborne and Rosedale Roads, Albany, Auckland 1310, New Zealand
(a division of Pearson New Zealand Ltd)
Penguin Books (South Africa) (Pty) Ltd, 24 Sturdee Avenue, Rosebank, Johannesburg 2196, South Africa
Penguin Books Ltd, Registered Offices: 80 Strand, London WC2R 0RL, England

LIBRARY OF CONGRESS CATALOGING-IN-PUBLICATION DATA
Cordsen, Carol Foskett
The Milkman/Carol Foskett Cordsen; illustrated by Douglas B. Jones.
p. cm.
Summary: In the early, early morning, the milkman makes his rounds, helping his neighbors in a variety of ways.
ISBN 0-525-47208-8
[1. Delivery of goods——Fiction. 2. Milk——Fiction. 3. Dairy products——Fiction.
4. Stories in rhyme.] I. Jones, Douglas B., ill. II. Title.
PZ8.3.C8167Mi 2005
[E]——dc22 2004021459

Published in the United States by Dutton Children's Books,
a division of Penguin Young Readers Group
345 Hudson Street, New York, New York 10014
www.penguin.com/youngreaders
Designed by Sara Reynolds
Manufactured in China • First Edition
1 3 5 7 9 10 8 6 4 2

First of morning, cold and dark.
Rooster crowing. Meadowlark.
Moon above the mountaintops.

Loud alarm clock. Snoring stops.
Mr. Plimpton out of bed.

Cream in coffee. Egg on bread.
Milkman jacket. Milkman hat.

Cranky pickup. Cranky cat.
Down the dirt road. Driving slow.

Windows open. Radio.
Country singer. Country song.
Cat meowing right along.

End of dirt road. Edge of town.
Cranky pickup slowing down.
Milk truck waiting. Loading fast.
Ice cream. Milk. Eggs.
Cat in last.

FAIRFIELD
FARMS
Fairfield
FARMS

Past the schoolhouse.
Past the park.
Straight down Main Street. Quiet. Dark.
Red light. Stopping.
Green light. Creeping.
Milkman humming. Milk cat sleeping.

HARDWA

Finally stopping. Orders ready.
Cat still sleeping. Snoring steady.
Double milk for Morgan twins.
Red house full of Kansas kin.

Next house empty. New folks soon.
Bensons left in early June.
Hope the Bensons like the Bay.
Hope the new folks want to stay.

Corner lamppost. Big blue sign.
LOST MY DOG. LOVE, CAROLINE.

Mr. Plimpton looks around.
Sees a shadow. Hears a sound.
Nearly misses house next door.
Painted yellow. Brown before.
Annie Gail just broke her leg.
Get Well card beside the eggs.

Mr. Richards. Out the door.
Early shift at grocery store.
Crooked sidewalk. Milk and cheese.
Curtains blow in morning breeze.
Corner lamppost. Big blue sign.
LOST MY DOG. LOVE, CAROLINE.

Mr. Plimpton looks around.
Sees a shadow. Hears a sound.

Yard sign last week. *Baby boy!*
Milk and eggs. And baby toy.
Ice-cream cups with wooden spoons.
William's birthday.
Big raccoon!

MAIL

Corner lamppost. Big blue sign.
LOST MY DOG. LOVE, CAROLINE.
Mr. Plimpton looks around.
Sees a shadow. Hears a sound.

Spiderwebs are full of dew.
Paperboy is almost through.
Sue and Nancy jogging by.
Mr. Plimpton calling, “Hi!”

CARROTS

Grandma Ellie pulling weeds.
"Buttermilk is all I need.
And ice-cream bars for Chris, my cousin.
White milk. Cream. And eggs. One dozen."
Mr. Plimpton looks around.
Sees a shadow. Hears a sound.

Next to lamppost. Under sign.

Lost my dog
Love Caroline
Milk

Lost dog home to Caroline.

No more houses. Orders filled.
Nothing broken. Nothing spilled.

Pickup waiting. Edge of town.
Dirt road.
Pickup slowing down.

Last stop, best stop. Cat jumps out.
"Daddy's home!" comes happy shout.

Milk
S
P
JAM

Hugging. Kissing.
Cat on mat.
Hanging jacket. Hanging hat.
Milk in glasses. Thanks are said.
Family breakfast.

Sun up red.